Balamory

B B C

Travel

RED FOX

TRAVEL
A RED FOX BOOK 0 099 48043 3

First published in Great Britain by Red Fox,
an imprint of Random House Children's Books
By arrangement with the BBC

Red Fox edition published 2005

1 3 5 7 9 10 8 6 4 2

Red Fox Books are published by Random House Children's Books,
61–63 Uxbridge Road, London W5 5SA,
a division of The Random House Group Ltd,
in Australia by Random House Australia (Pty) Ltd,
20 Alfred Street, Milsons Point, Sydney, NSW 2061, Australia,
in New Zealand by Random House New Zealand Ltd,
18 Poland Road, Glenfield, Auckland 10, New Zealand,
and in South Africa by Random House (Pty) Ltd,
Endulini, 5A Jubilee Road, Parktown 2193, South Africa

THE RANDOM HOUSE GROUP Limited Reg. No. 954009
www.**kids**at**random**house.co.uk/balamory

Illustrations by Red Giraffe   Text by Alison Ritchie   Designed by Clair Stutton

A CIP catalogue record for this book is available from the British Library.

Printed in Italy

Hello, I'm Miss Hoolie. I know you, don't I?

It's a work day in Balamory today, and Josie is coming to the Nursery to tell us all about her ferry trip.

Here she is now!

"Hello there, Josie!"

"Hi, Miss Hoolie. Gosh it's windy today! The sea is very rough, and the ferry was swaying to and fro, up and down and from side to side."

"You poor thing, Josie. I feel sick just hearing about it!"

"Well I'm fine now," laughs Josie, "but I've been thinking, I want to make my talk really exciting, so I'd like to tell the children about lots of different ways to travel."

"Great idea!" agrees Miss Hoolie. "Why don't you go and see Edie? She's travelled all over the world. She'll have some fantastic tales to tell."

"I'll go and see her right now, Miss Hoolie!"

So, which colour house will Josie be visiting first today?

That's right . . . the blue house!

"Hello, Josie. What can I do for you?" says Edie.

"Hiya, Edie! Well, I'm going to tell the children all about travelling today, and I thought maybe you might give me some tips!"

"Of course, Josie! I'd be delighted. Oh, what adventures I've had! Now, let me see . . ."

"Ah well, if you don't fancy floating in the sky, you can drift in a gondola on the canals of Venice. What a beautiful city, all that water, and no roads or noisy cars. Ever so peaceful!" says Edie dreamily.

"Sounds a bit too slow for me, Edie!"

"Well, if you want to travel fast, how about a kayak? Twisting this way and that through the water. I zoomed so fast down the rapids, I couldn't stop!"

"That sounds a bit too scary for me, Edie!"

"What about a camel ride in the desert then? Oh, that was a rocky ride, swaying from side to side!"

"I think I've had enough swaying for one day, Edie – on the Balamory ferry!"

"I know! You can race through the snow on a toboggan, from the top of the hill right down to the bottom, *swish swoosh swish!*"

"Yahoo! That sounds more like it."

"And you can go water-skiing on a lake. That's amazing! Just hold onto the rope and get pulled along by the speedboat. You can even learn tricks, like standing on one leg and jumping. You'd love it, Josie!" says Edie enthusiastically.

"Sounds terrific, Edie!"

"Wow, Edie. You really do know how to travel! Have you got any pictures I can show the children?" asks Josie.

"Only wee snapshots," replies Edie.

"Oh, I think I'll need big exciting pictures that all the children can see to help with my talk."

"Why don't you go and ask Suzie and Penny if they have any big posters?" suggests Edie.

"Yes! I'll go to the shop now!"

Josie arrives at the shop.

"Hi, Josie, what can we do for you?"

Josie tells Penny and Suzie all about her travel talk at the Nursery.

"I'm afraid we don't have any posters," Suzie tells Josie, "but we do have some water-skis."

"And a toboggan?" suggests Penny.

"Thanks! That gives me a brilliant idea! I'm off to the Nursery!"

Josie returns to the Nursery to tell the children all about the different

ways you can travel, and then . . . they all go water-skiing!

So, what was the story in Balamory today?

Well, I asked Josie if she would come to the Nursery and tell the children about her ferry trip.

Josie wanted to make her talk really exciting, so she went off to get some ideas from Edie.

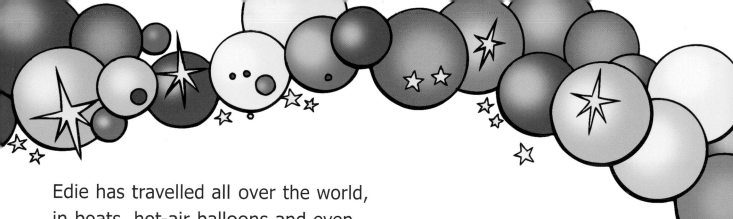

Edie has travelled all over the world, in boats, hot-air balloons and even on a camel! She told Josie about her adventures.

Josie went to the shop to find some pictures to show the children, and came out with water-skis and a toboggan instead!

Josie told the children some great travelling tales, and then we all went water-skiing! Everyone had a brilliant time!

So that was the story in Balamory . . .
    How many different ways have you travelled? Bye!